# GIANTESS GLOBALIST SPERM WAR

## MANDY DE SANDRA

# CONTENTS


PART 1                                              vii

Chapter 1                                             1
Chapter 2                                            10
Chapter 3                                            16
Part 2                                               24
Chapter 4                                            25
Chapter 5                                            31
Chapter 6                                            39
Part 3                                               47
Chapter 7                                            48
Chapter 8                                            54
Chapter 9                                            63
Chapter 10                                           69

Social Justice Warrior Snuff Film (Sneak Peek)       75
About the Author                                     83
Also by Mandy De Sandra                              85

# CONTENTS


PART 1    vii

Chapter 1    1
Chapter 2    10
Chapter 3    16
Part 2    24
Chapter 4    25
Chapter 5    31
Chapter 6    39
Part 3    47
Chapter 7    48
Chapter 8    54
Chapter 9    63
Chapter 10    69

Social Justice Warrior Snuff Film (Sneak Peek)    75
About the Author    83
Also by Mandy De Sandra    85

# PART 1

# CHAPTER ONE

I sit by the fire and study all their faces. The men barely talk. They are too young to have learned how. These are boys who have grown into men that only grunt or cry. Most of them know they'll be eaten. We wait for the giantesses to come for food and to choose their seed.

Eve Night is always somber. Some of the men fast, some binge, and some cannibalize. I am always tempted to eat the other men but I never do. The food the giantesses give us reminds me of the treats I used give the cats when I was a kid. They drop giant beige cubes that taste like cardboard and marshmallows. The aftertaste always leaves me nauseous.

Feeding my cat is the last memory I have before the bomb, before the brutal world where men became mites and women became gods. The men that can talk, share the story— they always do on Eve Night. I hear these tales each year, and what I can make out to be true is that it all began when a country that was called North Korea launched a new bomb.

I can hear the Neo-MRAs having their sermon in the

center of The Pen. They are sharing their own creation story. Some of it sounds familiar, but they're mostly wrong—except for the bomb. The leader of North Korea, Kim Jong Un, played a game of chicken with America's president. He dropped something biological that mutated our brains and our bodies.

They say this bomb killed 98% of the human race, that the winds blew it from America to the entire world. I can remember my parents, their bodies deteriorating and turning into ash as my body remained the same. I threw up and cried and held my cat while I stared at the ashes of the world I used to know. I was only five.

Everything I knew was gone.

Afraid to go outside, I stayed inside the house with my cat, Tonya. The toilet stopped working, the TV and Internet were gone. The power was out. Even the water was gone. We still don't get water, but the giantesses come and stand above the spiked thousand foot prison bars and spit on us. We drink it and wish for rain.

The giantess weren't always so bad, I was even saved by one. She picked me up off the roof of our house. I was afraid she was going to eat me. I thought she was an alien or a hallucination, but I saw more giant women. When she lifted me to her face, I recognized her. It was Mrs. Tivers, our local librarian.

She placed me on top of her shoulder, and I could see giant women for miles and miles. All of what was called Tampa was covered in human ash and giantesses. I can still remember a few tired and old giantesses leaning against the skyscrapers in downtown Tampa. They were crying and mourning their husbands and children but many of the young teenage ones looked happy. I could feel their anger and I saw blame in their eyes when they looked at me.

They blamed the men for the bombs.

Mrs. Tivers joined the other giantesses as they rounded up little boys, but when they saw an adult male they either stomped on or ate them. I cried as I saw fathers and sons scream in terror as they were eaten alive by nude giantesses. They gulped them down whole and sucked off all their meat, spitting out their skeletons like chicken bones.

The giantesses rounded up the boys who hadn't yet hit puberty. They placed us on their shoulders and they stayed perfectly still, until we heard a rumble and felt the ground shake.

I held on to her neck hairs and looked backwards, there were rows upon rows of giantesses that were in the thousands. They marched toward us, not like a military march, but more like birds making a formation.

When they reached us, the giantess who's shoulders I sat upon joined the front row and all the others followed.

The formation shifted like a marching band and the giantesses walked east. They didn't talk but I could feel them communicating. Their steps were perfect. It reminded me of Mrs. Thompson's science class when she mentioned that we only used 10% of our brains, and if we tripled that amount we could be telepathic. I stared at their faces and I could see them talking to each other with their minds.

The walk wasn't long, maybe thirty minutes if that, and for a brief moment I felt joy when I saw the giant Mickey Mouse ears in the distance.

The giantesses broke out of the formation and circled around Disney World. I squinted and saw how badly it was wrecked from the bomb. The rides were rusted but still looked better than what was left of Tampa.

The bombed out and rusted remains of Disney World became our new home. We had food and rides and shelter.

The giantesses stood guard. We couldn't leave even if we wanted to, but we were living in Disney World. It helped us momentarily forget about the horror we'd left behind.

One cloudy and chilly day, the giantess guards yelled in unison, "You have five minutes to get off the rides. We will be moving to the capital of our new world."

We scrambled, tumbling to the ground off moving rides. They turned around, dug their giant hands into the soil, and lifted Disney World into the air. We could almost see the clouds and feel the coldness of the sky. Hundreds of hands holding up the edges of Disney World.

I almost passed out when I looked below and saw the Pacific Ocean. The Giantesses breasts were barely above water. They would scoop up fish and give them to us for food and for water they would spit on us when it didn't rain.

We saw land on the third day.

There was a long stretch of beach and a blue flag with gold stars on it. The land was bombed out and desolate. The flag waved like it was saying hello.

The giantesses crushed the buildings that were left until we reached the mountains.

The Giantesses built spiked walls all around the field and we've been here ever since. I don't remember if it was us or them who named it the Pen.

It's so hard to sleep on Eve Night. I stay up and walk around the Pen. Shit, piss, and sweat everywhere. Different groups claim different parts of the Pen. Cults and gangs are everywhere. I managed to not join any of them.

The old religions are gone, but I miss them. I can remember my parents talking about Jesus. It's a distant memory now. Most of the Christian boys died, many Muslims committed suicide, and the Jews and Buddhists left their faith at Disney World.

The old gods have died. The giantesses are all we've got.

Now there's just lost boys stuck in grown men's bodies roaming around. When you're stuck with the same men, you see how much that doesn't change.

I stop my walk when I spot little Wilbur shaking in silence like he always does before Eve Night. I pat him on the back and say, "It'll be ok."

He barely acknowledges me, probably because he knows I'm lying. I keep walking and spot Kaz practicing boxing moves, and this guy Soys who's always selling crap to guys that are dumb enough to buy it.

I shake my head and keep walking, as if walking will give me some peace. I envy some of the guys who go full tribal, but I just can't be part of something I don't believe in. I don't believe in much, but I do believe something special happens when the giantesses choose you. Some of the Shaman in the Pen believe you get eternal life, some say when you're picked that you are just food, but I don't believe that.

I believe the men they pick are the seeds to bring new life.

I only focus on the giantesses and try to use the tools I learned in science class to find the closest thing to *truth*. When the giantesses visit, I study how they pick their food and how they pick a seed. The guys that aren't attractive, strong, smart, or sensitive enough become food. The men they pick as seeds have an extra variable.

Everyday I live in fear that I am not enough for them. I'm afraid that if I don't get picked by one of them I'll be their next meal.

These thoughts go around and around in my head as I walk near the Neo-MRA circles. I have to be blessed and baptized. They are the biggest tribe in the Pen. Word is that if you do not get the baptism before daybreak they will beat you to death. The Neo-MRAs are the men who know they will not ever be seeds, and believe that a day will come where *mankarma* will take down the giantesses and men will be free again.

Their sermons have been going on for two days straight, and they are the one group I will never cross. The only thing scarier to me than a hungry giantess is a group of men with nothing to live for.

The line is long but I get in the back of it as the Neo-MRA shaman preaches, "Be blessed, my brothers. Be baptized in the ashes of the fallen, their souls will merge with yours and a new world will be born—a world free of tyranny. A world with freedom and hope! If you are blessed and baptized you will bring forth that freedom we deserve. Be blessed with the ashes of revolution and rebellion against this misandry!"

I drift off as he goes on about how men will one day

reclaim their rightful throne.

The shaman stops his sermon when it's my turn to get baptized. He points at me. "You, yes you. You are what they want. You can be chosen. Whatever they do to you, whatever it is, remember how they have treated you. How they have treated us. Like cattle, the way farmers treated animals in the old world. Remember that and remember your brothers. Now be blessed in the name of revolution and spiritual justice."

The other shaman puts a black cross on my head and says, "You will be given new life and give birth to a new world covered in ashes."

The sun rises...

Damn it, how did I fall asleep. I feel hungover, like I drank fermented giantesses piss.

I wipe my eyes. The sun is too bright. No clouds. No rain. I stand up and stretch and see a group of Neo-MRAs laying on the ground.

They are alive but there's a weird smell coming from them. They remain motionless and I feel the sun disappear and a coldness crawl down the back of my neck...

It is the shadow of the giantesses.

"Brothers!" I see the head Neo-MRA shaman standing in front of the thousands upon thousands of men lying upon their backs. "From this moment, we will take our power back. Let our ashes become what we could never do."

The head shaman rubs two sticks together, creating the tiniest spark and flicks it upon the never-ending row of Neo-MRAs.

The flame sparks and spreads, covering each man in fire. Some scream, some laugh, but the shrieks from the giantesses drown out them out and the ground shakes.

A group of the giantesses leap over the spiked 100-foot fence and run toward the flock of flaming men.

They stomp on each man one by one, blood spewing and charcoaled flesh flying into the air, a few pieces even reaching the spikes on the fence.

It only takes the giantesses a minute to squash out the entire fire.

The rest of us stand as still as possible. I think about a nature show I watched with my dad, where I saw a mouse try to play dead, hoping the snake wouldn't see them. I can remember telling the mouse to run, but now I understand—when you are prey, you try to will yourself into invisibility.

A few of the giantesses lift their feet to inspect them. Not even a scratch. We have no power to stop them and I see the giantesses' eyes widen. That hungry look gives me nightmares almost every night. They are going to pick their meals, then their mates.

I want to stay still but I see a giantess starring right at Wilbur. She's nude except for a brown necklace made of jagged splinters.

Everything inside of me says to stay put, but something deeper and stronger forces me to run in front of Wilbur and scream, "Please Don't! Please, he's one of the good ones. Let him live."

The giantess stops and stares at me. Her long red hair covers most of her face, but I can see the green eyes through the red strands studying me. I expect to feel fear of death but I am overcome by her scent. The scent is coming from inside of her. It makes me want to be inside her.

She bends down and smiles at me.

"You are an actual good man," she says, as she reaches to her left and grabs a tall twenty-something with blond hair. She holds his feet like he's tiny violin and sucks off all his meat, flicking his bones to the side.

She burps and the smell makes me gag, but it doesn't overpower the scent of her body. I've never been this close to a giantess since hitting puberty. I can't move or even run. I am hers whether I want to or not. She reaches down and picks me up.

# CHAPTER TWO

She holds me carefully between her thumb and index finger. I feel like a rolled up cigarette.

She puts me up to her mouth and I cringe, fearing the worst, but I see open slots in her necklace—they are pockets about six feet deep. I look around and count ten slots around her neck.

Part of me wants to hide deep in the pocket but I peek out. The men are running. The best and bravest ones wait for their fate.

She kneels down and a guy I recognize stands proudly before her. She smells him and shrugs and then bites his body in half. His blood squirts all over me. I can feel his flesh slide down my legs.

She's not done and scoops up Kaz. I cringe, hoping he doesn't get eaten, but he lands in the pocket next to me. He stands up and I can see his face smiling. He reaches out to give me a fist pump but I can barely move.

Memories of war movies my dad would watch explode in my head, but they never showed the blood and bones.

I breathe a sigh of a relief.

I thought there was a logic to their selection process, but when she picks Melvin, an overweight bully who I've seen act like a horrible human being on a daily occasion, I realize it might be pure randomness. She places Melvin next to Kaz.

My giantess keeps passing on guys who are tall and well-built like me, but then she stops.

I peek over the pocket, straining my eyes to see why she is staring at mud, but then I see red eyes glowing from the ground.

It's a Singularity...wow. I've never seen one before. He's camouflaged, blending into the dirt.

She picks him up and the barely there sun bounces off the metallic parts of his body as she drops him into the necklace.

How many men has she picked up?

How many necklace slots are there?

She is walking at a fast pace but stops. I see another young man I recognize—Peterson. That's not his real name. He's a guy almost everyone likes, or at least no one hates. Even when the boys teased him about his afro and how his skin was the color of shit, he was able to talk to them and explain why they shouldn't say those things.

The guys started calling him Peterson, in honor of some guy who was popular and beloved by young men in the old world.

Anyone who said anything mean or hateful to Peterson would end up crying as Peterson hugged them and helped feel peace. He could have been the best shaman in the Pen but instead he just went around trying to build goodwill with all the groups. The Neo-MRAs wanted him to be one of them, but Peterson stayed non-aligned to any sect.

Here we are—the chosen.

I crouch deep down into the pouch and try to get ready for whatever will come next.

The giantesses have made their choices.

They form rows, side by side, and march toward the Pen's exit.

They step over the spiked fence.

I am outside of the Pen for the first time in fifteen years.

Everything is so clean.

I don't know if it is because of seeing only misery and filth inside the Pen, but the world out here looks beautiful. The giantesses gaze upon the lakes that glittering and clear and the skies that glow blue and bright. They walk across the lakes and I see towering magestic mountains in the distance. They look familiar, like I've seen them before.

Something with an S...Sweden...

"Hey," I hear from one of the pockets. I turn and see Melvin peeking out, "We've made it! I've heard so many stories about what happens. Look man, there is a shrine."

All of us in the necklace stare forward and see a sculpture of a giantess holding the globe and Melvin continues, "They are globalists!"

"What are globalists?" asks Kaz.

"Those who rule the world," says Melvin.

"Be quiet!" says our giantess, "or I will eat you all."

We stay silent but our eyes speak in the same way the

giantesses talk to each other. It's almost as if I can hear their thoughts about what the statue means, but even more intriguing are the fields of flowers surrounding the siren.

There are strange symbols across miles and miles of flowerbeds. Above the symbols tower the mountains. They are even taller than the giantesses and at the top of one mountain is an elder giantess.

The giantesses kneel before her and march left and right, walking to one of the many flowerbeds.

They each stand on top of flowers and face the elder giantess. She nods approvingly and says, "Let it begin," as fire explodes out of the mountain tops. "Release the men and place them to your breasts."

Our giantess take us out of her necklace and places us upon her breasts. Five men are on the left, and I am put with four others on the right. I stare at her beautiful face, but I struggle to focus on her because of the smell between her legs.

A couple of the guys turn around, and I'm pretty sure they're thinking about jumping off the breasts to go closer to what smells like the heaven the Neo-MRAs preach about.

"Turn forward," the elder giantess orders, "and look at me or I will destroy you with a glance."

We all turn around to face her as she continues, "You can't help your nature, even when great truth is to be shown to you your primal and destructive selves always win out."

"You have been selected for this moment and we have something important to show you," she calls out.

It sounds something like a bird or maybe a dinosaur,

and we see giantesses walking from behind the mountain, but they are holding little giant baby men.

The baby boys are fifty feet tall, some of them are being held, some are being breastfed.

The babies...oh my god...

But how?

"Yes, how?" the giantess says, "I can hear all of your thoughts. How indeed. Nature and technology have intertwined, to make a better world. The bombs that caused the mutation worked with nature making sure you would never be the dominant sex ever again. You are the last men of a leftover time, but you will have a chance to be reborn and to be better. We have selected you because we see worthiness in you. We understand we have been quite cruel and unfair to you since you've been little boys, but we will let you live out your childhood again. You are the boys that will be given a second chance to become new men."

I finally understand why we are so drawn to what is in between their legs—we are the sperm.

"Now drink from the bosoms, and don't fight one another for milk, for that time will come later," the elder giantess orders us.

We each get one drop, but it's all we really need.

It tastes so good. It's not just the taste that is divine-like, but it is how it makes us feel. It's so much better than those cardboard slices, but I get it now, the food they gave us was just dried and maybe spoiled milkish cheese.

I wipe my chin and lick the milk off my fingers.

Our giantess puts out her hands and signals us to get

on them. She stares down at us and says, "One of you will be my baby boy," she lets out a little smile and a tear comes rolling down and splashes us.

It feels like a large wave from the ocean.

I am the first one to walk onto her palm. I feel its warmth but a shudder comes over me when the other boys join me.

She places us by her feet. The sun is shining off her pink pubic lips. It glistens, surrounded by a jungle-like length of pubic hair. I can almost hear the lips speaking to me, saying come inside. Underneath those lips is her anus, with little stubbles of hair. We'll have climb them to get inside of her.

Our giantess lifts her head up while staring down at us. "My name is Darlat and I have chosen you. I plan to bear a son. We are able to do what we wish. There is so much we can now do. Our new selves can create life and our minds can manipulate our bodies, and manipulate many things. Nature has bestowed us with this power, because to be a giant is to be a god. We want life to go on, and believe that whoever gets to our eggs first will show they are the right man for our new world."

"So wait, we are like, going to go inside your vagina?" Melvin asks.

She nods and says, "Inside me, the worthiest and best one of you will reach the egg fist and become my newborn son."

"What happens to those who don't get there first?" asks Gerald.

"You shall die inside and become nourishment for me and my baby."

# CHAPTER THREE

The elder giantess blows out the fire on the mountain top and spreads her arms out like they are wings.

Our giantess smiles and lays her head back on the ground. The other giantesses do the same, and we look at each other, wondering what will come next, until we hear a song.

With their eyes closed, the giantesses sing a high hum in a language I've never heard in the Pen.

The melody is something you'd hear from alien birds. The sound makes the mountains vibrate but it calms us. The song slows down until it is gone and the giantesses are asleep.

I look up at the top giantess and she says, "It is time. May the most worthy reach the egg and become eternal."

She stands perfectly still, statue-like. Yet, I feel her glare, I feel the energy emanating from her mind.

She's connected to all of them, keeping them asleep and making sure they are ready. They all are connected to her, and connected to each other. They are more than giants, they are gods.

I look back at the vagina and then at the other men getting ready to run inside.

The biggest and tallest man drops down in a running stance. His long blond hair flows over his monster-sized shoulders. I recognize his face, but I don't know his name.

"To victory," he yells, and runs straight towards the vaginal lips. He jumps forward but falls on his back.

He sighs and says, "It's like sand paper. I can't push through the opening."

"You are too big," the shortest and skinniest of the guys says.

"Alright midget boy, you try," the giant blond hair man shoots back.

"It's Thomas," the short skinny guy snaps back.

"I'm Golden One," says the blond Viking proudly.

"What kind of a name is that?" snickers Melvin.

The men start to argue. I look around and see the other groups doing the same.

"Stop," I order. I feel all their eyes on me and tell them, "There's got to be a reason we are all together, why would they have more than just one guy?"

"Competition! They can't take away what is nature," Golden One proclaims.

"Maybe," I say, "But there will be no competition if we can't get inside."

"I'll get in and leave you losers behind," Thomas says, and walks over to the anus.

He uses the little stubble hairs of her anus like a rope ladder. He's not that strong but he is surprisingly agile and manages to slide over to the pink opening. He tries to kick in and swing through the lips, but the opening does not expand.

Thomas forces his arm through the tiny hole, but he

screams when it gets stuck. He struggles to take it out, and finally, as he pulls out his arm, the skin rips off and he falls twenty feet down to the ground.

He lands awkwardly on his leg and we hear a loud crack. He screams, bone sticking out of the knee, but before we can help him, Thomas is lifted up into the air. It looks like an invisible hand is carrying him to the mountains.

There are other injured men floating in the air. They float higher and higher, passing the giantess elder and then are dropped to the ground below. I hear screams and the sound of flesh being torn apart coming from the other side of the mountain.

"What happened to them?" asks Melvin.

"I think they are food for the babies," I reply.

"Damn, I don't want to be baby food," says Melvin.

More and more men fly over the mountain.

I look at the eight men in front of me. I've never taken the lead in the Pen. My way of surviving has been just to be cool with everybody and not step on anyone's toes.

I look at the guys and say, "Ok, let's pause for a sec. If any system is going to work it's going to involve us working smart and working together."

"That sounds stupid," says Melvin.

"Nah, he's right," says Kaz.

"Who made you leader," Golden One retorts, "I should be leader."

"Let's worry about who's leader once we get through the vagina," I say. "Look, the only guys I recognize are

Peterson, Kaz, and Melvin. Who's everybody else? I'm Tyson."

Kaz holds up his hand and says, "I'm Kaz and I agree with Tyson."

Peterson nods in agreement and says, "I am Peterson. Who are you guys? What are you good at?"

A man in his mid-twenties with a beard and curly hair and an average face and frame says, "I'm Avery, and I don't even know why she picked me. But I am here and I want to be a baby again and become a giant man. I'll do whatever I have to do. Right now I think we do have to work together."

I nod. I don't see Avery as a threat.

I scan the circle and notice a man who looks very feminine, he has a way about him that reminds me of the giantesses. The feminine young man nods shyly and says, "I'm Michael L."

"Michael L, or Michelle?" I ask.

"Both," Michael L says and shrugs.

"Michelle doesn't belong here with us," says a man who almost seems to blend into the shadows. He steps forward and we see he has red eyes and mechanical parts attached to his arms and legs.

"You are one of the singularity guys!" Kaz says. "I've heard of you but never seen one of you. I thought it was just a rumor."

"I'm called Robert," says the robotic young man.

The oldest guy there, a 27-year-old with short brown hair and a shit-starting smile says, "Whoa, you are like a poor man's RoboCop. Singularity, damn, it's real." I don't even know who RoboCop is and most of the others don't either. He continues as we stare at him in confusion, "I'm Soys and I got the knowledge. Before the bombs, I'd sneak onto my dad's porn sites and entered a bunch of reddit and 4chan chatrooms. That's my skill and that's probably why these giant bitches picked me."

Once again, I am drawing a blank on these references, but Soys continues, "All that stuff was basically like a really dope health class, I know how to get that pussy to open. Homeboy Tyson right here is right. We are going to have to work together.

I never knew anything about sex, but Soys spends ten minutes explaining everything: how vaginas work and how they expand and get wet so objects can go inside them. He tells us the different erogenous zones and how just little touches and licks in those place can do so much.

Hearing all this, I see how off the Neo-MRA sex experts were.

With a whole new world of knowledge, we stare ahead, knowing what we need to do, but are scared to actually do it. The lips look intimidating and the anus stubble looks scary.

"Let's do it," Soys says, "Tyson, you're the button pusher, Melvin and Avery—you're going first."

They don't want to go but the group picked the weakest to go first. Some things don't change even outside of the Pen.

The two young men walk together and we watch with fear and anticipation.

Both men stand face to face with the anus and Melvin says, "Aw man, it kind of smells, why do I have to do butt stuff?"

"Do it, or I will break your leg," Robert says, his red eye brightens with rage.

Avery shrugs and says, "It can't taste any worse than the cardboard breastmilk bars they feed us," and licks the anus, putting his hand inside of it, going in and out and licking all around.

"Fuck it, just don't forget this when we are all inside," Melvin says and follows Avery's lead, licking and fingering the anus.

We watch in awe and can feel the moisture building inside the vaginal lips.

"I told you it would work," Soys says staring at her private parts. "But that vagine is not ready yet for us to slide in. Let's get our Cirque Du Soleil on and get up in there."

No one knows what he means, but we get into the formation that Soys and Robert designed. Soys says the button, or what is called the clit, is the most important part to stimulate. He gave me the job because I seem to be most level-headed, have a good feel for things, and very strong arms.

Golden One kneels down and says, "Get on top, Tyson. I will prop you up with great pride to press the button to open the competition up."

I nod and climb on top of him.

I've seen some of the boys play chicken fights in the pen and break bones. The giantesses would come and eat them out of mercy. I never played, but now I wish I did.

Golden One begins his climb using her hair stubbles, his strength definitely makes him a necessary part of the team. The others follow behind us, climbing through the pubic hair as each guy finds a spot by the lips. They start slowly, with light licks and soft touches.

I look lower toward the anus and see Avery looking freaked out and Melvin's leg is sticking out. The other half of his body stuck in the anus.

"Pull him in and out," Soys says while licking what he said is called the vulva, but he says he likes to call it 'the meat flaps.' "Direct anal stimuli will get her even more wet."

Avery looks happy to no longer lick her anus and does his best to pull Melvin in and out.

Golden One reaches high enough for me to massage the clit with my elbow. The moisture builds into a frothy batter and I feel the sweat dripping down my cheek.

"Don't use your arms," Soys says, "use your head and go in circular motion. Put your fucking head into it!"

I circle my head on the clit, the wetness sticks to my hair and I grind harder. I can feel the button part starting to expand, and one of the guys below yells, "It's getting slippery, it's working."

Another one yells, "It is, I see it expanding."

"I'm going in first, boys," Soys yells.

I look down and see Soys climb to the opening and slide head first through her vagina like it's a waterslide.

The other boys do the same, climbing up and sliding forward through the wet, glistening lips.

Golden One taps me on the back to signal he is dropping down. I grab onto the pubic hair and climb behind him. He stretches the hole a little bit and a pleasure sigh buzzes out of our giantess' unconscious mouth.

I'm ready to go in but I hear someone calling, "Tyson, wait, we need help getting up."

"We need you to take us up," Melvin says, wiping all the feces from his head and torso.

I look back at the vaginal opening and I can see it is

starting to tighten again, and I only have one hand I can use.

I hate this moment, the unfairness of this choice.

Avery is useless, but I know Melvin Neo-MRA sympathizer and won't be able to bring anything but problems inside.

"Avery give me your hand," I order. "Melvin, I'll get you next,"

Avery doesn't even wait to consider what I said, and jumps up and grabs my hand. I use all my strength and swing him into the opening. He barely slides through. I can feel the moisture leaving and I say, "I am sorry, Melvin."

I slide headfirst and hear Melvin cry out, "It's all fucked up. It's not fair! The Neo-MRA's will make sure these whores are turned into ashes!"

# PART 2

# CHAPTER FOUR

The outside world is gone and now we are in her.

I expected darkness but there is light. All of us gaze in awe at the never-ending tunnel of electrical currents shooting back and forth.

The men get into a running stance, but Soys says, "I don't think all of this is just to see which one of us is the fastest."

Golden One scowls. "Maybe you lie, Soys. You just say that because you know I would win."

"Actually I'm probably the fastest," I say, staring at the electric currents flowing from front to back, lighting up the vaginal walls. "This is like a computer, almost a like circuit, and that means it's more than just a tunnel to the egg."

"Computer, vagina, race. All the same. Competition," Golden One proclaims.

"I know," I say, "But right now, we don't know what the hell is in that tunnel or where the egg is, or how any of this works. The more we stick together, the more of a shot we will have to reach it."

"Do you think there are times when no one reaches the egg?" Kaz asks nervously.

I have no answer for Kaz, but Michael L says, "Empathy, guys, use it. What do nature and women think about us?"

"Nothing good," Peterson says.

Michael L nods. "It clearly thinks we are shit and probably wants to make it as difficult as possible for reproduction."

Avery nods. "That makes sense, but we can't just stand here either."

"We have to move forward," I say, "But we have stick together, at least until we reach that Cervix place Soys talked about."

"Fine," Golden One says, looking at Avery, "You are weakest, you walk ahead. Ten feet ahead. We do that on hunts, same rules as Pen."

"What the fuck, no!" Avery exclaims and stares at me.

"That's not right," I say. "We need to leave the Pen rules outside.

"You don't want to win?" Golden One says looking confused.

"I do."

"Then make tough decision act like führer."

"Fine," I say. "I will walk ahead, but then I am the leader."

"Fine. Deal," he says.

We keeping walking through the electric cave.

I trust my eyes less than I trust my scent. The more

we walk the more the scent calls to me. Each step is close the egg.

I notice something coming up on the walls—I squint and see there are little bumps but they almost look like a language.

I walk further and see that it is on the ground too.

"What is this?" I ask the guys.

Soys is the first to come up and check it out. "I don't know, pussy bumps or nerve endings. They look kind of creepy."

I get closer and inspect it. I recognize that these aren't bumps but a language that is through touch. "It's a form of braille," I say.

"What's braille?" Soys asks.

"What blind people read."

"Can you read any of it?" Soys asks.

"No," I tell him. "You have to touch it to be able to read it."

I reach down and press down and try to see what it says.

It cuts my finger but I don't stop touching it...but then the wall stretches itself out like a screen. The red liquid expands into a type of etch-a-sketch, spreading out on the vaginal wall.

I get teary eyed. The blood sketch is me as a baby.

My face looks like when I was two.

The giantess appears in the blood sketch. It shows her holding me and giving me so much love as I get bigger and bigger until I am her size and we live together forever in love.

"They are changing the whole life cycle," I say, "And it's beautiful. Put your hands down her braille and see your future with her."

All the guys walk forward and touch the tops and the bottoms of the bumps.

Their blood is the key, it mixes with what is probably is her DNA and shows their future together.

I study the men's faces when the blood appears. I've never seen such happiness in any boy or man's eyes. But seeing themselves as babies takes away the joy I feel for them—if that happens, then I am dead and my life really had no point.

Michael L is the last guy to go. He presses his finger down to read his fate, but bliss does not appear on his face, only fear.

The blood turns into fiery red image of the giantess, bathed in blood, holding Michael L as a bloody baby.

She looks at Michael L. with anger. I can feel the heat of the blood getting warmer. Michael L lets out a tear but the flame doesn't care—it stretches out like a wave and turns him into ash.

The guys jump back and duck down but the flame is gone.

"What the fuck just happened?" Soys asks.

"I bet he had something," Kaz says, "Something she could feel in his blood."

"She acted like red blood cells," Singularity Robert says. "My data calculates they have evolved psychically, where the mind can project its defenses. I am 88% sure of the case," Robert says. "I detect the giantess psychic blood cells are 95% effective."

There is no time for a moment of silence, no time to reflect on our fallen friends.

There is only fear of what comes next and knowing there is no second place.

The braille is still there, closing in on us. It's almost as if it is measuring tape, to see if we reach a certain height.

Except for Avery, all of us are six feet tall or higher. The vaginal braille rubs against our heads. It almost feels like fingers rubbing against a lamp to make a wish.

I look back and see the guys have smiles of pleasure all over their faces. The braille feels so good against our heads and feet. It's almost like she is trying to have foreplay with us. Everyone looks happy except, Avery, since he can't reach the top even when he stands on his tiptoes.

The ground starts rumbling.

Her body is unhappy about something.

It's Avery, she doesn't like that he doesn't measure up.

But then why did she pick him?

Something in my gut tells me there's more to Avery than being undersized.

"Golden One," I say. "Pick Avery up and carry him."

"What?" Golden One says, but notices the floor by Avery is starting to shake.

"Help me," Avery begs. "The floor is getting all fucking weird, because I can't hit certain spots."

Golden One shrugs and continues to walk forward.

I run back, pick up Avery, and put his head up against the top floor of the vaginal wall.

The vaginal floor slams down where he was. It expands back normal as I hold him up with all my strength.

Avery does his best not to cry, but he does, feeling the ridges rubbing against his head.

"They feel like love, like you are worthy enough to be

in the world. Like you are truly good enough, but it's a lie," says Avery.

"Just throw him down," Golden One says with his back to us. The rest of the guys follow and I'm left to hold him up, but I wonder if Avery wants to even go on.

"Avery," I say, feeling a bad strain in my arm. "Stop fucking crying, be grateful you are here, and act like you and me could be in the final two."

"Ok, ok," he says, as I walk forward and hear him whisper to maybe me or maybe himself, "I'll be the final one."

I worry my arms are going to give out but I see that the braille stops and the vaginal wall goes back to its normal cavelike size.

I rush forward and let go of Avery. There is pleasure in resting my arms but more pain from missing how the braille feels.

"What the hell was that?" I ask the guys.

Soys smile and says, "I'm not totally sure, but I'd say we just passed the G-spot."

# CHAPTER FIVE

We carefully walk forward.

Even Golden One timidly inches forward.

I keep wondering if I did the right thing by saving Avery. It feels right but from the standpoint of surviving and replicating myself—it feels like self-sabotage.

We keep walking in silence until Soys says, "I'm one of the few guys in the Pen who watched porn and I've got mad knowledge on 4chan and Reddit. I watched a ton of porn and noticed all the dudes had big dicks and I read on these sites about how women want to bang dudes that are a certain height. These bitches might be bigger and have psychic bodies, but they are still the same. They still want the big D."

Kaz nods while catching his breath, "Unless height just means that you have the genes to be giants too. That would make sense."

"Nah, bitches are just shallow," Soys says.

"So where do you think we are now?" I ask.

"I'm trying to remember the diagram. This Roosh guy shared it online. I can remember his beard but it's hard to remember what is after the G spot. I do remember him saying it's important to hit it, which it looks like everybody did except little-ass Avery."

"Fuck you, man."

"Technically we are fucking this giantesses together," Soys says and laughs.

"Focus, guys," I say, "So Soys, what do you think is after G spot thing?"

"I don't know for sure," Soys says," "But I remember in Reddit/PUA, guys saying that big dicks can reach the A spot, so the girls know you are there."

I nod and say, "Let's be careful and keep a look out for the A spot."

The guys nod silently and stoically, but I can feel how scared everyone is, even Robert has an air of fear about him.

But we walk forward.

It's a silent and somber march, everyone is careful with each step, but we jump when we see something different than the usual electric current flashing across the sides of the vaginal walls.

"What was that?" Kaz asks.

No one can answer when we see the sides contort and twist.

It looks like there are men in the walls. Dead ones who are now moving.

"Whoa...is that where you go if you don't make it?" Avery asks, more amused than scared.

"Maybe," I say, noticing they are pushing forward and more men inside the wall are appearing. They push through the skin on both sides of the vaginal wall to block our path.

One of the men inside the wall tries to punch Robert.

The wall stretches as his fist flies out, but Robert ducks just in time.

The pink neon wall stretches out more, and another man near Robert tries to grab him. The Singularity boy dodges them and uses his metal arm to slam the guy backwards from blocking his path.

"Yes! This is true nature," Golden One sings and punches all the men back into the walls that are near him.

Avery shadows Golden One, who is the only one enjoying that vaginal wall as men are trying to kill him.

Kaz is boxing them, throwing left and right jabs and knockout uppercuts.

Are these the loser men who have been reanimated psychically, like zombies from the gianteeses' mainframe to work as her protectors? Or just manifestations of our own minds?

I duck a punch from a vaginal wall man and grab onto one another man in the wall to use him as a shield—he feels like a human being.

I don't want to end up as one of these men. I can feel the rage and misery pumping through its blood. I knee it in the balls but it doesn't stop. I probably either have to beat its brains out or overpower it.

It lunges at my throat but I block it. I try to push it back but it's stronger than me. No. I can't lose. I picture the blood child of me and her holding it and I let that feeling push me forward.

I harness it and push him back to the wall, and cock back my right fist. I punch it as hard as I can in the face.

It vanishes back into the wall and I run forward to the others. There are no more men in the wall but the ground in front of us is no longer solid.

Soys is the only one laughing and grossed out by the liquid puss that stands in our way. It's a little pit about six feet long but I have no idea how deep.

"There's nothing funny about that," I say.

Golden One stares at the other side and says, "I am strong. This vagina, it about strength. I jump now."

Golden One runs forward to the ledge and jumps over the gooey white mucus landing on the other side with a few inches to spare.

"Come on, you fools!" Golden One says. "We must go forward."

Kaz shrugs and backs up and then runs as fast as he can, leaping over the pit.

He lands on the other side and looks back at us. "Long jump is my game, you Americans never did this stuff in your gym classes."

Robert shakes his head and says, "I do not like that goo," and in disbelief I watch the metal in his legs stretch and extend to the other side.

"Whoa!"

Robert keeps his back to us and says, "The giantesses use the technology of their mutation and bigger brains, but they cannot forget the technology man invented. Their next step in evolution will be Singularity. Giant-esses Singularity. It has a nice ring as non-singular humans say."

Soys rolls his eyes and says, "Dude, you are fucking human. Cut the bullshit. You are just a poor man's Inspector Gadget."

Once again we do not get the reference, but Soys

shrugs and says, "Peterson, why don't you make the leap. You probably can make it."

There is doubt in Peterson's eye. He's not as strong and agile as most of us. He gets down on his knee and looks like he is praying.

"Who the fuck are you praying to?" Soys says in disgust. "How do you still believe in a God? I thought you were supposed all smart and shit, Peterson."

Peterson looks up from his prayer. "I was praying to myself," and runs fast and jumps forward.

He just makes it, but his feet tremble and it looks like he is going to fall backwards.

"Lounge forward, and fall on your stomach" Avery screams.

But Peterson does a back flip summersault and lands on his feet.

"Damn bro, you could have been the first black guy in Cirque Du Soleil," Soys says and then looks at me and says, "Why don't you go next, Tyson. I don't mind going last."

"No, after you," I say, studying him and seeing that there is excitement in his eyes about the mucus sinkhole.

"Okie dokie," Soys says, and walks to the pit. He stares down. "I got bad knees. Twenty seven year old knees in the Pen, might as well be old man knees. So I am going to take my chances in here."

Soys winks at me and does a belly dive into the mucus. The white ghostlike ooze covers everything but his head. He walks forward in the middle and then stops. He doesn't scream, doesn't do anything. He turns perfectly still, almost like the elder giantess.

Avery just shakes head at Soys' stupidity and says, "Thanks for dying, Soys, you at least gave me life for another few minutes," and jumps on Soys' head and then jumps to the other side with the other men.

Soys still doesn't move but I can see his face's reflection in the white mucus water. His face looks so peaceful. So happy. So serene.

I think about what he said about his knees and that is bullshit. Soys could have easily made that jump. I've seen that guy doing leg lifts of 200 pounds are more.

He knows something we don't know...

I risk it and jump into the mucus...

It feels even better than the braille. My God...I don't believe in one but this feels as good as being touched by God.

But it's her and I feel her.

This must be like what it was like to kiss a girl and know love in the old world.

The mucus wraps itself around me and I can't move.

I am lost in this perfect moment until I hear Soys say, "You guys might be strong but you aren't smart. Pussy mucus is a good thing, it's like the opposite of a cold. It's what happens when she cums. We just took a cum bath, and nothing bad can come from that."

I look at Soys and says, "I don't want to leave."

Soys gets out and joins the others. "Then don't."

I remember why I am here and force myself out. The mucus falls off of me but I can feel it on my skin. There is a glow emanating from myself and Soys.

Golden One stares at us. "I want cum bath too!'

He tries to jump into the mucus, but he cannot break through. He tries again but it's like he is hitting an invisible wall that he can't break through.

He stops and looks in sadness as the mucus dries up looking like an ice skating rink on top of a swamp.

We keep walking on and I can feel the guys looking at Soys and me with anger. But I feel a primal wrath toward them too—I want them all to die so I can reach the egg alone.

"What the fuck are you thinking about, Tyson?" asks Soys taking me out of my thoughts. "Cause, I am thinking some cool shit, some smart stuff. I think we got a leg up on these losers."

"Something like that," I say.

Golden One stops and says, "You two speak another word of this, and I will break both of your skulls against each others, then you won't be so fucking smart."

Robert scoffs, "Vaginal mucus is no match to the Singularity."

"Yeah, yeah, Tin Man," Soys scoffs, "Let's focus. We need to get past the A-Spot."

"What's the A-Spot again?" Peterson asks.

"A spot in the vagina that is hard to reach," Soys says. "Some people deny it's even there, but I've seen pornos. Big dicks hit the A-Spot, that's why those bitches scream so hard."

Avery points ahead. "Is that it?"

We look forward and see a mountain type block that lifts the vaginal canal up to about five times its normal size. It looks like the canal goes back to normal on the other side.

It reminds me of the mountain the elder giantess stood upon.

We get closer and see plant-like objects growing out of the fleshy hill. They are beautiful and horrifying. They are made of flesh and act no differently than vines or the blackberries that spring up at the end of summer.

"This looks pretty simple," Golden One says, "We climb. Strong men get over, weak stay behind. Muscle is the big dick now."

Golden One starts climbing. He digs deep into the mound, trying to avoid the artery looking veins and bushes, but to move up he grabs one of the veins near the top. He swings to go left but the vein breaks off. He uses the other vein to stay on the mound.

He looks back and smiles and says, "See strength is what wins in the..."

His voice breaks when the veins jump out of the mound, before he can even fall down to safety, they wrap around him like a bunch of snakes joining together to strangle its prey.

"Hee...lp," he begs, but we don't.

Golden One's face turns bright red, until his head pops off and his blood and body is absorbed into the flesh of the vaginal wall.

The vein vines recoil, except for the one that Golden One broke off. It disintegrates into the vaginal floor and I feel my stomach drop down to my feet.

# CHAPTER SIX

"I'm not really going to miss him," Soys says and shrugs.

"How the fuck are we going to get over that?" Avery asks.

Peterson looks at Soys and says earnestly, "Hold my hand."

"What?" I ask, confused.

"Just hold my hand, man," Peterson begs Soys.

"What is this gay nonsense?" Soys shoots back.

"Please," Victor begs.

Soys rolls his eyes and grabs Victor's hand.

Peterson grips it tight and says, "The mucus, it makes it so that you can easily climb. You will grip tighter to the mound. You are rewarded for being brave, for being willing to drench yourself in her...." Peterson takes his hand back from Soys to touch the wall and says, "Shit, it doesn't transfer."

"What's with the meat garden?" asks Kaz.

And it all clicks and I say, "That we can be strong, brave, and smart without tearing the earth apart. All of this, all of it is just tests to see if we are worthy to be her child."

"Whether they want it or not, this world shall be our domain again," Robert says, and runs to the wall and extends his arms to the top.

He reminds me of a movie I saw with my dad, where the villain had six mechanical arms and could climb buildings. The hero could shoot webs. I can't remember the name. There are so many things I can't remember from that time.

"I don't have singularity arms," Avery says to me. "I'm not going to make it unless you let me climb on your back, Tyson."

"Let me see if Soys is right," I say, and walk up to the mound. I place my hand on it, and the mucus on it acts like a suction cup.

Spiderman...that was the name of film...the vaginal mucus makes me like him when it comes to climbing.

"I can carry one of you guys," I say and look at Avery. "I'll pick the lightest, it is only fair."

Kaz shakes his head in anger and Peterson says, "I can do more than Avery."

Soys walks up to the mound and says, "I'm taking no one," and easily climbs over.

"You fucking asshole!" Kaz yells.

Soys gets to the top and says, "Nah, just smart. Good luck choosing, Tyson."

Kaz and Peterson look away from the mound and focus their anger and fear at Avery. They look at each other and then stare at Avery with violence in their eyes.

"No!" I order. "It's not time for that yet, and if you fucking touch him, I will take none of you over."

"That's fucking dumb," Kaz says. "At least chose between me and Victor. That at least makes sense."

"We aren't putting anyone to their deaths until we are near the egg," I say. "We don't know what is behind that mound. I also don't trust the guys who are already over there. For now, we need each other, so instead of picking, we're going to do that Cirque du Soleil stuff Soys was talking about to get over the mound. We can be a human bridge. I'll be at the top hanging down and each man climb above the other."

"So we make an alliance," Kaz says. "Fine. Works for me. I'll let shorty and Peterson climb to the other side on my back. I'm cool with that."

Peterson nods and says, "I'm cool with it too."

Avery has no other choice and nods his head.

I climb quickly up the mound. I recall the Spiderman movie as I hang upside down with my feet sticking to the top. Kaz is tall enough to just reach my hand and holds my arms while putting his legs out like the bottom of a ladder.

Avery goes first and climbs quickly over our bodies and jumps down. I hear him yell out in pain when he hits the ground.

Peterson goes next and goes up even faster.

Kaz follows right behind and then I muster up all my strength. I flip over and crawl down to see Soys and Robert angry to see us all.

The anger leaves Soy's face and he says, "Well, at least we'll have a crew for when we hit the cervix."

I notice Avery is still on the ground holding his rib, but

the other men are looking forward while squinting their eyes. Except for Kaz, as he stares at Soys with hatred.

"Can you see it?" Soys asks Robert.

"Yes, and it concerns me greatly," Robert says.

I look away from Avery and try to see what they are talking about. It's looks like the same tunnel, but then my eyes notice a white electric current that is swirling around what looks like an exit. The swirl in front of the exit looks like a force field. A mind in itself. Little electric currents that are capturing the shadows of the cave we travel through.

"Fuck!" Avery screams, "I think I broke my fucking rib."

"Fuck your rib," Soys says. "We got more important things, like figuring out what the fuck that is."

"Tough it out," I tell Avery, knowing that compassion has to be kept to a minimum now.

Avery stands up and holding his side and looks forward. "Well isn't the next thing the cervix, maybe that is it."

"Maybe," Soys says.

"Maybe shut the fuck up," Kaz says. "You are a fucking liar. You knew that shit and let us almost fucking die."

"It's called being smart you dumb fuck," Soys shoots back.

I feel angry at Soys too as we get closer to the swirling center. I try to let this feeling go, but awful thoughts churn around in my head, like throwing Robert and Soys into the force field.

Is this force field the cervix?

I wish the bombs dropped after I took sex-ed.

But this is more than just basic biology, it's deeper.

Every obstacle is a test and we have to pass it. Men are always focusing on how to fix something, but so many times I've seen them never try to find out what the right question is.

It's frustrating, not knowing, and the other are starting to feel not only angry at themselves but angry at each other.

A memory bubbles up, it's my father telling me that women are a complicated puzzle you'll never figure out, but the one thing they always hate is when you get mad.

Maybe the question is easier than I thought.

I need to get rid of this feeling of wanting to kill most of these guys.

I think of my mom's yoga videos, how the music was always relaxing, and I try to feel what the bliss will be like of being a baby again. I let that feeling take over and dominate and subdue my thoughts and my body.

I breathe in, I breathe out, and leave the anger behind about Soys, the world, and try to become the love that my future mother and wife wants me to be.

Peace comes to me, just enough of it, that that I feel no fear and walk through the force field-cervix.

As I turn around I hear a punch connecting with someone's jaw.

There is blood dripping down Kaz's fist and a smile on Soys' bloody face. Kaz then looks at Robert and throws an uppercut at his jaw. A mechanical shield covers the face of Robert and Kaz says, "You are a piece of shit too, tin man. You two don't deserve to go past the cervix."

"Stop, Kaz!" I say, trying to stop the fight.

"Don't tell me what to do, you are just going to try to kill me later," he says, his face getting redder by the second. "This whole world, the whole everything, is fucked. It was fucked before the bombs and it's been even more fucked after the bombs…"

"Seriously stop, your face…" I say, "harness that anger for later. Please! The anger and hatred it's…"

"Fuck that, Kaz," Soys says, "go ahead, I'll give you another free punch. Come on, you know I'm just going to kill you later."

Kaz swings, and when he connects to Soys' right eye, Kaz's head goes blood red and pops off, and a voice says behind us, "Hatred and violence is not welcome past here."

The vortex-cervix is the giantess in psychic form.

She stands in front of us at our size.

"My boys, my loves," she says, and flicks her red hair. She is wearing all white, the color of all colors.

"Is this your soul?" Peterson asks.

"Something like that," our giantess says, looking at us. "This was my height before the bombs, this is my inner self, you could say."

"Isn't that a term for a vagina, so that would be kind of redundant," Soys says and looks backwards at us and whispers, "it's called negging and that Rosh guy says it works."

The giantess looks at Soys and says, "Such little faith, such great disdain for us women. That is what got us all to this point. But I've seen goodness and smarts and adaptability in your eyes. Come to me and let me show you that I am love."

Soys can't resist and goes right to her. She kisses him.

Her body merges into his and Soys glows with his eyes closed.

The kiss and glow ends and he stumbles across where the force field once was.

She smiles and says, "He will make a good son and husband," and then turns around and tells Soys, "You need to learn to make friends."

She turns her attention to Avery and smiles. They are the same height. "You have something special, don't you, something above the physical? What is it? I guess we will find out. You aren't my type, you shouldn't even be here, but here you are because I felt your specialness. Let me kiss you and know your soul."

He goes to her and they kiss. Avery looks happy for the first time, his face not full of pain and worry. She lets him go and he walks forward.

Peterson smiles at her and a little tear comes out of his eyes.

"I like you. Strong, sensitive, gorgeous, and a good heart. Come to me my son, kiss me and know my love."

Their kiss is full of passion. It's painful for me to watch. It ends, and Peterson walks forward looking like he's found God.

I want to be next and taste her lips feel her *soul* but her eyes are on Robert. Her eyes widen as she studies him. Her look is detached. Clinical.

"You are the next evolution of man, aren't you?"

Robert nods.

"You will either rot or flourish if you make it to my egg."

Robert stays silent and she comes up to him and kisses him.

She stops and says, "You are still very human...are you

human enough? I don't know, but it would be interesting to find it out."

Robert still does not smile but a type of contentment is on his face as he walks forward.

She looks at me.

I stare back into her eyes and wish we could have met before the bomb. She puts her soul-colored fingertips through my hair, caressing it and whispers, "I want you to win. I want you to be the one but I have no control from here on out. Be you and don't be scared and you will be with me," she kisses me and I am at one with her, knowing a love that I I am now willing to kill for.

# PART 3

# CHAPTER SEVEN

She is gone.

The area past the cervix is smaller but yet it strangely feels safer. Her words keep playing again and again and I can feel a change in the air—in the vagina and in the other men.

Suspicion and jealousy—I can smell and feel it in their eyes and in their steps. I know because I have it too. Did she whisper that to all of the men, or just to me?

Avery stops for a moment to catch his breath and says the mantra, "Pain isn't real, but her love is real. Pain isn't real, but her love is real."

"Both are real," Peterson says, "but it's worth feeling pain to feel her love again."

Soys nods and says, "I know I come across as an asshole and I wish you guys a violent deaths before we get to the egg, but a love like that, if I would have felt that in my life—I'd be a different person—I'd be a better person."

"It is not love," Robert says, "It's only that her superior genetic code will be given to us and we can surpass nature's crooked and cruel game of survival and replication. A singularity giant would be the idea of god coming true."

"Jesus Christ, Robert," Soys says, "That's disenchanting as fuck. Keep that nerd shit to yourself, let us enjoy and ponder this...poetic possibility for just a moment you metal face fuck... what about you, Tyson? You are the only one who doesn't look like you've been pumped full of Prozac."

I assume Prozac is something that makes you feel good. "I feel what you guys feel, I just don't focus on it. I want to focus on getting to her egg."

We walk further and further until Avery says while gritting his teeth through the pain. "What do you think life will be like as a giant? What do you think we will do all day?"

"Who cares," Soys says. "We will be out of the Pen and sucking on those giant titties."

"Couldn't get that get boring, though?" Avery asks.

"You are boring, man," Soys says and laugh. "It sounds perfect."

"I guess it will be," Avery says.

"Computers do not get bored," Robert says. "They are aligned with the purpose of existence, to be alive and to be efficient, creating more and more memory."

"Jesus," Soys says. "I hope this Singularity shit never happens."

"It has and it will," Robert says, looking forward at the vaginal canal that is turning into a metallic mirror. "The canal is Singularity..." he pauses and stares at himself in the mirror. "I don't recognize myself, so strange, but so much better."

I pause and see myself...

I want to cry.

The age.

The stress and the hurt in my face.

I haven't seen what I look like in over a decade. The singularity cult were the only ones who had the anything of technology…

Damn, I look so old. I look so beaten down. I look like if I don't become a baby again I'd be better off just dropping dead. It's like the mirror is talking to me, telling me to stop and quit and just end it, that I should die here and now, and die by choice instead of by failure.

I look back at Soys who looks nauseous and says, "I don't think what we are seeing in the mirror is real."

I look away from the mirror and her words come back to me. The mirror, it's a way of looking into our own souls and pushing out our demons, to showing we can defeat them.

But I don't want to see whatever it will show next. I turn away and try to walk, but I can't move. It's like without the mirror I have no kinetic energy to push me forward.

I open my eyes and look at mirror. My feet can move, but it's horrible. Reflecting back to me is my face melting and the others eating my arms for susistence.

I turn away from the mirror of torture and look at the others.

Soys is gritting his teeth and sidestepping left to right saying, "Test me, baby, I'll pass every one! Keep it coming. I get the game and I know you want me to win. Show me the worst you got!"

Avery holds his broken rib and cries, forcing himself to stare at the mirror and trudge forward.

I could only imagine what horror the mirror shows him, probably reminding him that he shouldn't even be here. I have to look back at it, but instead I turn my eyes onto Robert. He just stares and walks forward repeating the mantra, "Lies, lies, more lies, falsehoods, falsehoods, and even more lies."

The only guy not moving is Peterson, who screams, "The world really is worthless. No life should be here. They are right, they are right!" and starts slamming his head against the mirror.

My own fears stop and I fear more that Peterson could hurt her—if the mirror breaks, will she?

I run to him, facing images of me being strangled to death by Soys, and grab Peterson by the neck so he'll stop slamming his head into her mirror.

But he he's stronger than me. Better than me in so many ways, but that goodness and strength is making him too weak, too unhinged.

He's trying to grab my head to slam it against the wall too.

A tear drips out of my eyes, like my emotions know what I am going to do.

My hands take over and grab his neck and twist.

Snap.

The cracking sounds echoes throughout the vaginal tunnel and with sadness and horror I stare down at the corpse of Peterson and say to him, "Sorry, I had to, I really did."

His body looks peaceful and maybe even happy. Maybe death is better than life, but I know that's bullshit as the floor below him starts sucking down his flesh until all is left is his skeleton.

Death.

That's the worst fear and the only one that is true.

I stare back at the mirror walls and force myself to walk.

The mirrors end and the smell of her is stronger.

We are closer to egg and it's intoxicating. Her essence, it's like oxygen to me now.

Soys takes in the smell and smiles. "I believe we are reaching the uterus. I can smell the ovaries. The eggs, boys, they are cooking! We made it through. Man, those mirrors, they even took out Peterson, that fucking pussy, surprised you made it, little Avery."

"Fuck you," Avery says, but then smiles and breathes heavily through his nose. "The scent takes all those images away. I can smell the egg, it's everything."

Robert nods and says, "After visual torture, we get the pleasure of scent to show us we are worthy. To show us where we go."

"Man, you would have been a great TV announcer," Soys tells Robert sarcastically.

"I am television and so much more," Robert says back, "and I will be pure Singularity once I am birthed again."

"Yeah, yeah," Soys says and looks at me. "Didn't know you had that in you, Tyson. You are probably now in the front running. She wants you. If we were smart we'd all you kill you right now. Don't you think, guys?"

Avery holds his ribs. He is the only one who has my back, but he can't do shit.

Damn it, killing Peterson could lead to me being killed now. I can try to fight off Soys but I don't know if I could take him. Soys is staring me down but Robert's arm stretches out and pushes Soys back.

Robert mechanically turns his head at Soys. "Until we reach near the egg, our highest probability is to have a group of three and one human for a shield. Always go with highest probabilities, always."

"I never fucking liked math, and I don't like aspy fucking nerds," Soys says starring down Robert. "But you are probably right, tin man."

Robert looks directly ahead. "I could end you both right now, right this second. You stand no chance of harming me without a technological weapon."

Avery nods. "He's right, he could kill all of us right now. So instead, let's just walk forward and make it to the end of the ovary."

# CHAPTER EIGHT

Silent steps go on and on until we feel something like wind, and we look down.

"Oh fuck," Soys says.

It is a heavy drop into what looks like acidic water.

"This is why I wanted more people here," says Robert. "I cannot find an applicable solution, there is no logical one. This is quite perplexing."

"You don't say," Soys says, and stares forward squinting his eyes to make out what's past the acid. "I can see it, that's the Ovary, and the Fallopian tubes. It's all there, guys."

I stare ahead and see the tubes that look like the water slides that were at Wet N Wild. I nod and say, "We are so close, I just want to leap over there and somehow get there."

"Why don't you?" Soys asks.

"That is a mathematical impossibility," Robert says.

"No shit, but that's the problem with you aspy robotic guys, no heart, and especially no balls."

"Foolishness," Robert says, "But there is a solution,

that only logic will show us, but even I can not perceive or see the solution at this second...this is quite frustrating, and I do see now that even though the female humans have evolved in size and brain, they are still quite fond of the illogic."

"You're right," Soys says. "They haven't changed, they still want the same shit. Dudes with balls who aren't afraid to kill and die for them. They are just fucking taller than us now."

Roberts looks confused. "I don't comprehend,"

"I'll show you and her, that I have the balls," Soy says. "I'll will my way over. I will jump to her and leave you behind," and he jumps with such certainty in his eyes that ends when he begins to fall.

In a millisecond, he turns around, begging Robert to extend his arms.

Robert's arms fly out and catch him two inches way from the acid.

"Fuck, fuck, fuck, I fucked up, pull me up, please pull me. Pull me the fuck up. I don't want to die!"

Avery shakes his head in anger. "You should let him go."

"He is turning into an unknowable variable, which I do not care for" Robert says, "but statically we are better off...or...are we? This dilemma does not have a statistical probability or solution...in more human terms. I don't know what to do."

"Lift me up! Just lift me the fuck up!" Soys screams.

"Keep him there," I say, watching him dangle, not enjoying this but trying to see what went wrong and where he might have been right to take the leap.

The phrase he said, *I'll will my way* over rings sort of true. There has to be a way to get there and it doesn't take special powers, but it can't come from ourselves. We aren't special, we really aren't, but the Giantesses are...

"You did right thing, but you did it backwards, Soys," I say."

"That doesn't even making sense, pull me up Mr. Roboto!" Soys begs again.

I don't even bother trying to tell him it's not balls she wants, but a connection. Trust. And Faith. Faith, in her, faith in becoming one. Faith that I can do anything through her.

I touch the ground and focus on what she told me. That faith is what will get me to her.

I picture a ladder that could cross over the acidic drop, and then using that ladder to climb to her, and be able to look into her eyes. A ladder so long and sturdy, I could walk past anything.

"Please," I tell her in my head. "Please give me a way, I have faith in you."

I close my eyes and go the ledge and step forward. I feel the ground beneath my feat and lose my fear.

"How? Impossible," I hear Robert say.

I open my eyes and keeping walking on mid air but feeling the ladder with each footstep.

"Mother fucking Indiana Jones, bro, I should have saw that—a pussy egg is the holy grail," Soys says and screams, "Now, swing me up, swing me up now!"

I stop and say "Swing him up and walk with me. Just have faith in her, not yourself, that she will give you what you need."

"I get it now," Avery says, and I can hear his steps behind me. I hear Robert's clunking feet walk on the air with Soys swinging below us screaming in fear.

We reach the other side and I can smell something

like the ocean. It is dark but I can feel water near us, I look backwards and see Robert dangling Soys.

"Ay shit, damn it," he says. "Come on Robert, what about the odds, or whatever, the more men for the Fallopian tubes the better."

"No it will not be," Robert says.

And before I can even plead, Robert drops him into the acidic pool.

He dissolves and is gone in seconds.

As much as I thought Soys was a shitty guy, there's now no balance of power against Robert.

His red eyes look right at us. For someone so emotion-less it's so easy to read what he wants.

"Don't kill us," I say, "Do it for her, show her that you can be compassionate."

Armor wraps around his body, but there is not point, I can't take him out.

Robert covers himself with battle gear. "The odds are in my favor with 96.3%, but even 3.7% is too much to chance. But, I have deducted that showing pathos and unselfishness, though extremely flawed when compared to logic is a principle she embodies and therefore I must as well. To her, my Singularity and calculation can be a weakness, so I shall give you some compassion," chains shoot out of him and wrap around us.

We are stuck together and can't move.

Avery laughs and I let out a loud sigh of frustration.

"I must be in line with pathos, logos, and her ethos. I shall win but I am sorry that you will lose. I can imagine that death and failure causes great despair. There is now no way that you can now win, my percentage of winning is 98.7%. I can't honestly say it was enjoyable to know you, but Tyson, you were an above average player, and with your last breaths you can feel proud that you helped the Singularity begin. Good bye."

And then he's gone.

Already in the Fallopian Tube and I hear the sound of him swimming and it's not putting him on the fritz.

Damn it...he's right, there's no logical way I can beat him...yet a tiny amount of faith remains that I can still beat Robert an feel all her love.

I can't get out of these chains. No strength, no escape, no nothing, just the tight steel. Where the hell did Robert hide this in his body and does any of this even matter anymore?

It doesn't matter.

I look at Avery for help but he sits in pain, the steel pushing down on his ribs. There is so much pain in his face. Whatever specialness I felt in Avery it's not coming out now and it might have never even existed.

Each moment, each second we sit here is Robert getting closer to his new life and our death sentence.

I try to slide out but my hands are in the way. I try to recall her touch, her kiss, everything that gave me those few moments of bliss. I push my wrists hard against the chains.

"What are you doing?" Avery asks.

"Something you don't have in you, but I do," I say and scream in pain when I feel the bones break in my wrist, palms and fingers.

"AGGGGHH!!!!!" I scream, sliding out of the chains and doing everything I can to manage the pain.

The chains drop off him, but fear grips me because he might see me as dead weight.

"I can't believe it, you did it..." he pauses and stares at my broken wrists. "You saved me twice, I owe you...and there's no way I can take him out alone. Can you do anything with your hands?"

I just scream in anguish.

"I'll take that as a no."

I put my worthless hands and arm to the ground. I can't feel anything. They are starting to go numb. "One of us is getting to that egg before that walking tin can does. Let's go."

"Alright," he says.

I remind myself the pain won't last but death will. I put the hurt out of my mind and fill it with the promise of her love and walk forward until we are in the tubes.

"We gotta to go fast," I say.

"The metal, it could slow him down."

"Then we better go now...use me like a surf board and steer. It will get us there faster."

"What if you drown?"

"Then at least I die doing my best trying to win," I say and get on my stomach.

He gets on top of me and I take one huge breath and he pushes me forward into the tube.

He holds on tight and I feel him directing me, as we fly forward.

The water is rocky. It reminds me of the white river rafting my dad used to do. I wanted to go so bad, but my mom said it was too dangerous.

They were right.

The water splashes hard to our left and my head hits hard against the left side of the fallopian tube. I feel the blood gush out of head, but I take a quick breath and Avery directs us back to the middle.

We slide left to right, going faster and faster, but when I look forward there's a white block, looking like an iceberg.

Avery pulls my body sideways and we stop in front of it, and the tiny bit of hope I was holding onto is as gone as my hands.

I try to make a fist to punch it but I only scream in pain.

"Lean against it with your skin. You're probably burning up. It's the only thing that I can think of," Avery says.

He's right but by the time it melts it would be too late. I shake my head and say, "That could take hours, we don't have hours."

"That's all we can do. It is the only solution we got right now unless she removes it herself."

"No," I say through the pain, "this is a test. It's all fucking test."

I put my body against it and the feel cold. The ice numbs some of the pain, but the ice almost starts to feel warm.

Avery puts his body against the iceberg and I can feel it starting to drip down.

"It's working," he says, "I told you. This is the weakest iceberg ever."

"It shouldn't even have been here, but if her body acts like a computer...I guess she needs an area to cool it all down. Like an air conditioner."

"Whatever, keep it going...get mad...anything that will heat up your body."

I only have to think about how Robert is probably approaching the egg now and I let the rage travel through my body. I stare at my reflection in the ice, I spit on it, and the ice cracks and I see something in the middle. I wonder if that is like an engine or something.

We have to be so close, come on, just melt, just melt, and just maybe, he hasn't gotten there and I still have a chance.

Water drips down as the ice melts faster, but inside the block I hear something engine-like, almost like a chainsaw revving up.

"You hear that?" I ask.

"Yeah, what is that?"

"The black inside of it...it is still blurry. I can't make it out, I think it's like a computer main frame...it's the size of a..."

The ice block cracks into a bunch of little pieces.

We duck down and are covered ice. I try to push myself out of it, but my hands don't move and I can't breathe.

*Please* I beg to the giantess, *please take me out of this and just give me a chance to be the one.*

*Please.*

I feel something or someone grabbing my feet and taking me out of the ice. It's not her, it's only Avery and I see a horrified look on his face and a very sharp thick piece of ice in his hands.

He points the ice at the pile and says, "Look, his body is in there. He looks pretty dead," I can barely breathe and see, but I assume it's Robert.

He looks back at me and points the ice spear at my

neck. "I don't have any choice. I'm sorry, Tyson, but you're right I am special and I've always been the one for her. At least you saw it. So I'll make it quick."

I let out a tear and prepare to accept death and a life that will end in complete meaninglessness, but before Avery can stab me to death a metal hand punches out of the ice behind him.

# CHAPTER NINE

Avery points the icepick away from me, and we both turn around to see Robert.

Not even a scratch on him. It looks like he's just rebooted.

There is a shredder type device on his hand that looks pretty strong but not strong enough to cut through a fifty foot block of ice.

Robert doesn't even bother looking at me. It's like he's calculated in his mind that I'm no longer a threat, but he stares down Avery. It's strange, there's almost a fear in Robert's eyes, but Avery has none—he looks confident for the first time.

Robert runs away from Avery.

I stand up and look ahead and there is it is—it's like a blue bubble of electricity and warmth. The smell is spirituous. I step toward it and even feel less pain staring at the beauty of the egg.

Oh, that smell, it reminds of when I smelled an orange for the first time. It has sugar and vitamins—I smell everything I need in that egg.

But Robert is getting closer.

I'm about to scream. I feel so hopeless seeing only Avery is close enough to stop him, but Robert turns around and stares down Avery.

I run to them but Avery turns around and holds his hand up at Robert who remains motionless.

"You were right," Avery says, his voice is different now, less full of fear, less weak, less...him. "I am special but it only works in special moments..."

Robert charges at Avery, but Avery stands tall and closes his fist and Robert falls to the ground.

"Malfunction...impossible," Robert says.

"Nope," Avery says and smiles. "The giantesses know there some like me, those with a smaller mutation, and I am one. I can simply manipulate any technology, any machine, which makes me better than all of you."

"Impossible," Robert pleads. "There is no data, no causality. No..."

Avery laughs and swipes his hand right and Robert is flown against the end of the vaginal wall.

Robert looks frightened, but then a human smile emerges. "Singularity shut down, power off."

Before Avery can do the final kill, Robert's red eye goes dark and the metal parts of his body drop to the ground. I pause and wonder which guy I should team up with.

They wrestle each other down. Robert is bigger and appears stronger but his muscles are weaker than Avery's.

Avery gets him a chokehold and I realize this is my only shot. I swallow down all the pain and run as fast as I can to the egg.

I run right past them.

I can smell and taste the ecstasy of what is so close to me."

30 feet.

20 feet.

10 feet.

5 feet.

I can almost touch it with my broken hands...

But a metallic hand grabs my left arm and pulls me backwards. Surprisingly, it doesn't hurt, but the pain of not making it to egg is the worst pain I've ever felt as I slam against the vaginal wall.

Everything is blurry but when my vision returns I see Robert's right metallic arm is hovering above me...

It comes down on me again and beckons me to stay still. In disbelief, I see Robert himself is armless.

His other arm is in the air and holding Robert down, while Avery stares at me, keeping his hands in the air to control both of Robert's arms.

"Fuck," I can only say with despair.

"Yup," Avery says. "So close, so damn close, Tyson. You probably are the most deserving, but it's not going to be you."

I try not to succumb to giving up. I try be computer-like, I search my mind for any weakness, any way that I can make things even, any way to make Avery screw up a sure thing...

I get an idea and tell Avery, "Robert is the most deserving one. He has strength, good genes, the right size, and like you can manipulate machines. He's better than you. You shouldn't even be here. Robert is what she really wants."

"This is correct," Robert says.

Avery's eyes expand in rage and I watch Robert's arm fly to his mouth and stuff themselves down his throat. Electric sparks and blood shoot out of his body until his red eyes and his whole body dies.

The arm hovering over me falls, and Avery tries to use his powers but they don't work.

Avery lets out an annoyed laugh slip out and says, "You are smart and perceptive, I'll give you that, Tyson. Stronger and taller too, but two broken arms, thank you for that. I genuinely feel grateful to you...I've never killed anyone with just my hands, but now, I just don't have any other choice. And to be honest, I am going to kind of enjoy it."

I feel fear.

I feel anguish.

But I don't feel pain.

No pain at all.

Is my body prepared for death?

Does it already know that it is over?

Avery walks over and all I can do is try to kick as a way to defend myself, but it's futile. He just walks around my legs and stands above my head.

"Kneel before me and I will make your death quick, and then I will savor that beautiful egg."

Fear shoots through my veins and I grip my hands butI don't feel pain. I feel strength. I don't understand...

Avery stares back at the egg. "I can feel it, you can too, it really does have magic. The bombs, it gave women and men like me who were considered weak, magic. Guys like me are going to be the giants and men like you are going to be stomped..."

He lifts up his right foot and slams it down fast on my face, but my arms lift and my hands stop it.

"What the fuck..." Avery says.

I hang on to his leg and flip him over. I put my hands around his neck and squeeze. "The egg is magic, just being near it heals you."

Avery's eyes go as red as Robert's once were and his arms weaken until they collapse by his side. And he's gone.

I put my finger on his neck just to check, but nothing is going on inside of him.

I stare right into his dead eyes and never want to be like him. He doesn't look peaceful or any a better place, just dead—a failed life that will be forgotten.

I stand up and stare right at the egg.

This moment is finally here as I begin my walk to paradise.

I savor each little step. I take in the scent and how being near the egg heightens all my senses.

There is a tingle I notice on my forehead right were they put on the cross on me.

She really did heal me.

She really is a god.

Being able to walk instead of run, I see the true beauty of the egg: electric currents creating a ball that looks soft and secure. All of it controlled by her mind, body, and if it exists—her soul.

The steps add up until I can touch it for first the time.

Bliss.

Pure bliss.

And before I can walk inside, the electric currents shorten to my size and she appears. "I thought you'd be the one," she says, her blue and electric skin is so beautiful.

"I thought so too," I say realizing that I am actually flirting, and it feels so normal, so pre-Bomb. So right. "I am here, I really am."

"You are here, and so am I. We have learned how to astrally project ourselves to receive new life, and to create it. I can't wait to show it all to you, and raise in you this new and better world."

"I want to be part all of it."

"Then kiss me and let us begin."

I do.

I kiss her for real this time and I savor it. I take in every taste and every touch. I need her. I need to be inside of her. I need to be reborn inside of her.

"I'm ready for you," she says and her essence is absorbed into the walls behind us, and I stare at what is front of me.

The electric currents that were protecting the egg are gone and I see the egg—it's white and glows with wonder and love.

So pure, so perfect.

In the white I see one little opening, it's just my size and I know instinctively know what to do.

I step forward and enter the hole. I feel bathed in white and her face appears in the egg, "You are about to lose consciousness. You are about to be reborn, and I just wanted to say I love you and always will."

The white all around me falls like rain onto me, and I stare into her eyes.

They look so happy, she's about to say one more thing, but then horror appears on her face and she screams as the white turns into black ash.

# CHAPTER TEN

And the black ash spreads and spreads and spreads and spreads and spreads and spreads and spreads and spreads and spreads and spreads and spreads and spreads and spreads and spreads and spreads and spreads and spreads and spreads and spreads and spreads ands spreads and spreads and spreads and spreads and spreads and spreads and spreads and spreads and spreads and spreads and spreads and spreads and spreads and spreads and spreads and spreads and spreads and spreads and spreads and spreads and spreads and spreads and spreads and spreads and spreads ands spreads and spreads and spreads and spreads and spreads and spreads and spreads and spreads and spreads and spreads and spreads and spreads and spreads and spreads and spreads and spreads and spreads and spreads and spreads and spreads and spreads and spreads and spreads and spreads and spreads and spreads and spreads and spreads and spreads and spreads and spreads and spreads and spreads and spreads and spreads and spreads

What just happened?

What is happening?

I can barely breathe now, there is too much ash in the air.

I feel myself falling....

Her body is deteriorating into ash, until the ashes catch my fall and push me upward.

I want to scream. I want her voice to comfort me but I don't feel her presence anymore. The electricity is gone and her ashes push me up further and further into the sky.

The ashes are everywhere.

And all I can think of is the baptism on Eve Night, it's the same color and has the same smell.

No!

No!

No!

Please, no!

Let her live, let me be at one with her and become part of her.

But it doesn't matter, no matter what I beg, she is gone and I am only left with her ashes.

The ashes come to a stop and the dust clears.

I stand up in shock on the top of the ash that is probably over 500 feet in the air.

The ashes cement below me, and the wind blows the other ashes all around.

I stare at all the men standing on top of grey mountains made of dead women.

The breeze takes the ashes all the way to the top mountain where the elder giantess looks on in horror until she dissolves into the black ash as well.

When the ashes touch the baby giant boys they dissolve into nothingness. Their cries echo off the mountains until they are gone, along with their voices. The bomb that made them was taken away by the bomb the Neo-MRAs made.

It was all hidden in black cross that they baptized us with, but it wasn't a baptism, it was an undetectable STD to bring about the genocide of all the giantesses.

Through the horror, a voice emerges below of a man screaming, "Men, we did it! We destroyed them. The giantess globalists are gone. Nature's cruelty is gone. Life is gone and it is beautiful."

All the men in the Pen have escaped and are below us cheering.

Hymns are being sung and the leader carries on, "Yes, sing and rejoice. We have made the prophecy come true, and we can spend our final days as free men where our worth and value won't be judged and we can celebrate that failed experiment of humanity and giantesses. We can live however we want and die not at the hands of beasts and whores, but as boys who can now be free men!"

Cheers from below reverberate off the mountains.

But all of us looking down stay silent...

We can only look at each other, left to right, mountain to mountain with rage in our eyes, but not as much as the sadness we feel about the rest of our lives.

All of us, the "winners" who will live with the greatest loss we'll ever know.

The men below all kneel down and make signs of the cross, worshiping us.

In this new world without giantesses, men are already finding new idols and gods who stand on top of what we knew of love and purpose that is gone and replaced with a hate that stares down on a world preparing to die.

SOCIAL
JUSTICE
WARRIOR
SNUFF
FILM
4.95
MANDY DE SANDRA

# SOCIAL JUSTICE WARRIOR SNUFF FILM
# (SNEAK PEEK)

## Chapter 1

Dr. Gerald C. Peters was sick of doing cable TV interviews. He was drifting off, tuning out another newscaster asking the same damn questions.

He continued doing them only to boost book sales and Patreon subscribers. His wife hated them because they always led to a flood of hate mail arriving at their house. The constant threats had him losing sleep. They called him a racist, a NAZI, a sexist rape apologist. He knew in his heart he was none of those things the vile post-modern Marxist said he was, but yet when the moments of tiredness crept in he'd wonder if he truly was and if his own Johari Window was keeping the truth from him.

The interviewer aggressively snapped her fingers to get his attention and the feminist reporter repeated, "Do you think toxic masculinity exists and what do you say to those who believe that you are the father figure to a new generation of angry and sexist young men?"

"I think the media needs to delve into its Johari Window of darkness."

The reporter mockingly laughed. "Doctor Peters, I'm an educated woman, but I don't know what you are talking about. Wait... is this some kind of Jungian slang?"

"Not educated enough. It was founded by researchers Joseph Luft and Harrington Ingham."

"Of course this comes from two white men named Joe and Harry."

"I don't see what their race and sex has to do with a theory."

She smiled politely until her producer spoke into her earpiece and she made his Wikipedia definition her own, "ah Johari Window, it's been awhile since I've brushed on my Psychology 101."

"It's a fascinating study and shouldn't be forgettable."

She paused and adjusted her earpiece and smiled. "Yes it is...well then, you must know that the 4th Window panel is what you can't see. Your blind spot, the darkness...The darkness in your own heart, many would say your blind spot that reveals itself in all the problematic and harmful things you say about women, minorities, and non-binary people—people who don't have the privilege or safety of being a white rich male who profits on pain and anger and dividing an already divided world."

Dr. Peters shook his head in annoyance and looked at her like a Chess player looks at children playing Checkers. "First, I don't know who is Googling and telling you Wikipedia summaries in your ear piece, but no one can see the 4th Window panel, except God. And how dare you spout such dangerous rhetoric!"

"You are the one comparing feminists and non-binary people to Maoists & throwing red meat to a fanbase that loves to bully and torment minorities and women online."

"Grow up."

"Excuse me?" the woman said aghast. "Are you going to tell me go clean my room as well?"

"You and those trying to silence free speech, grow...up...because you might feel triggered when it comes to disenchanted young men taking their anger out by tossing around third grade insults online, but there is a killer going after people like me, who just want to have uncomfortable dialogue."

Her face went red and the snark in her stare vanished. "Dr. Peters, let me say right here, this news program has denounced The Antifa Snuffer, Or SJW Jigsaw. We at FNN news do not believe in violence, even against vile human beings."

Dr. Peters scoffed. "And yet you cover him or her, or 'they' as it likes to be called. The media, you and all your lackeys are responsible for emboldening him to make his...videos. Especially, you Miss.."

"That is dangerous and slanderous to say," the reported retorted.

"Well now you know how it feels. Not fun, huh kido."

"You got me there, Dr. Peters...you got me there."

***

Dr. Peters continued to wait in the green room for the second security detail to show up.

Out of morbid curiosity & annoyance, he stared at the FNN news showing talking heads wondering who SJW Jigsaw was, though Dr. Peters found that name to be hokey and false—this killer didn't need a pop culture reference, he/they was a snuff film making menace, murdering and torturing anyone they deemed problematic & influential.

The ANTIFA Snuffer was the most appropriate name for him. That was exactly who this man was who went killing YouTubers and fellow colleagues of the Dark Web.

Whenever the SJW Snuff Filmmaker was in the news, Dr. Peters always got a knot in his stomach, the same feeling he had in his twenties at the library when he wanted to talk to a girl he felt was out of his league, and ended up reading Jung instead. He'd later learned the knot was actually his ego—a mix of biology and psychology adhering to the laws of nature that man and lobsters followed. But this knot was not ego—but fear of not being able to survive if the ANTIFA Snuffer found him.

The knot tightened when Dr. Peters watched two images appear on the screen. One of a plump forty-something YouTuber called Sarfon of Anatole & a problematic has-been provocateur named Cooked Antarctica.

Dr. Peters always thought Cooked Antarctica needed therapy and maybe to have a religious experience to cleanse him from his meth using tendencies, but he considered Sarfon a friend and a fellow moderate trying to keep boys from joining the alt-right.

Peters swallowed his sadness and anger and watched the screen change back to the FNN reporter.

"A new torture video has appeared, it is being labeled as Social Justice Warrior Snuff Film #6...what you are about to watch is a truly deplorable act of men. They might be deplorable themselves but do not deserve to be tortured like this...if you have children or are easily triggered by violence please change the channel."

They never do, thought, Dr. Peters, no one ever changes the channel.

The screen switched to the infamous Kickstarter doll-Non-Binary-Bobbi holding an iPhone. The doll stared back at the camera. The iPhone turned on and a scrambled high voice issued forth, "Even after the prior videos, these problematic video & radio stars still continue their hate speech. They call us cancer but they are the cancer... I apologize for my ableism to those who are suffering with actual cancer.

No, the intolerant cannot be reasoned with. They have become NAZI machines of hate and they will only stop if they know the flame will come for them..."

The camera panned away from the doll onto the faces of dried tears of Sarfon of Anatole and Cooked Antarctica. They wore NAZI outfits that had shit smeared on them.

Dr. Peters shuddered with nausea, he could almost smell the feces and the piss rising from the screen.

"There are no moderates, liberals, or conservatives when it comes to intolerance. All are equally evil," the voice behind the camera said. "Their flesh must be cleansed of their sin of hate before they enter Mother Earth."

"No, please! I only dressed like a NAZI for the lol's," Cooked Antarctica begged. "I'm an artist, bro, I'm just a meme...I'm sorry. Please don't, man... I mean they, I mean... And I hate architecture, I hate the fucking wall idea, I was totally joking."

"Hitler was an artist and architect too," the ANTIFA snuffer's voice retorted stoically. Their hand reached out in front of the camera holding a flame torch pointed at Cooked Antarctica's face. "You play with fire, it's only fair that you get burned."

The flame sang out of the torch hole, a high hissing sound that was drowned out by the screams of Cooked Antarctica. The flamed swirled around the left side of his face until flesh dripped and oozed down, joining the piss and shit on his shoes.

Dr. Peter's couldn't believe they weren't censoring the violence.

Cooked Antarctica's weak chin bone looked like a charcoaled chicken bone. His burnt to a crisp eye hung by a thread until it unraveled and fell inside his cheek as it rolled around like a pinball in a broken machine.

Dr. Peters shed a tear, not for Cooked Antarctica but for his friend, Sarfon, who believed in the same values and was going to burn at a stake for them.

An advertisement for refinancing mortgage showed at the bottom of the screen and Sarfon shook his head and cried, already accepting his fate.

"Send money to my Patreon for my fam....iiiiioo," and the flame covered his whole face, and Sarfon screamed for a God he had never believed in. The flame ended and all that was left of Sarfon on Anatole was puss bubbles and skull bone stained with burnt blood.

The camera stayed on the faces of the dead YouTubers and the voice behind the camera spoke, "I will make one final video to crystalize my message and make sure no more fascists and intolerant evil people will feel safe to speak their hate. We will achieve true anti-fascism..."

The tape cut off and the camera focused on the shocked reporter who sputtered out, "My God..." she took a few seconds and her reported persona returned. "We apologize about not blurring the content...we will take a break..."

A commercial for Norwegian cruises played and Dr. Peters turned the TV off to say a prayer for his lost friends and for himself.

Mandy De Sandra is a Gnostic Goddess who has inhabited the author Christoph Paul's body to give her message of Gnostic Chaos Sex Magic for the early 21st century. She sometimes enters the body of Kanye W. as well but doesn't like wearing red hats.

# ALSO BY MANDY DE SANDRA

Kirk Cameron & The Crocoduck of Chaos Magick

Ravished by Reagansaurus

Fox News Fuckfest

Gay Zombie Sluts in Key West

David Foster Wallace's Footnotes F'd Me in the Butt

Social Justice Warrior Snuff Film